COUNTY CUP 5

CUP GLORY

Also available by Rob Childs,
and published by Corgi Yearling Books:

County Cup series
1: CUP FAVOURITES
2: CUP RIVALS
3. CUP SHOCKS
4. CUP CLASHES
5. CUP GLORY

Coming soon:
6. CUP FEVER
7. CUP WINNERS

Soccer Mad series
FOOTBALL FANATIC   SOCCER MAD
ALL GOALIES ARE CRAZY   FOOTBALL DAFT
FOOTBALL FLUKES   SOCCER STARS

SOCCER MAD COLLECTION
includes SOCCER MAD, ALL GOALIES ARE CRAZY

SOCCER AT SANDFORD
SANDFORD ON TOUR

Published by Young Corgi Books:

The Big series
THE BIG GAME   THE BIG WIN
THE BIG MATCH   THE BIG PRIZE
THE BIG DAY   THE BIG KICK
THE BIG GOAL   THE BIG CLASH
THE BIG BREAK   THE BIG CHANCE
THE BIG STAR   THE BIG FREEZE
THE BIG FIX   THE BIG DROP
THE BIG SEND-OFF

THE BIG FOOTBALL COLLECTION
includes THE BIG GAME, THE BIG MATCH, THE BIG PRIZE

THE BIG FOOTBALL FEAST
includes THE BIG DAY, THE BIG KICK, THE BIG GOAL

THE BIG FOOTBALL TREBLE
includes THE BIG BREAK, THE BIG CHANCE, THE BIG STAR

Published by Corgi Pups,
for beginner readers:

GREAT SAVE!
GREAT SHOT!

ROB CHILDS

COUNTY CUP

Book Five
SEMI-FINAL STAGE
South v East

Cup Glory

Illustrated by Robin Lawrie

CORGI YEARLING BOOKS

COUNTY CUP 5 : CUP GLORY
A CORGI YEARLING BOOK : 0 440 863872

First publication in Great Britain

PRINTING HISTORY
Corgi Yearling edition published 2000

1 3 5 7 9 10 8 6 4 2

With thanks to the pupils and staff of Northolt High School for their
help in the preparation of the cover.
Football kit on cover provided by Pro*Star ®

Set in 12/15 pt New Century Schoolbook by
Phoenix Typesetting, Ilkley, West Yorkshire

Corgi Yearling Books are published by Transworld Publishers,
61–63 Uxbridge Road, Ealing, London W5 5SA,
a division of The Random House Group Ltd,
in Australia by Random House Australia (Pty) Ltd,
20 Alfred Street, Milsons Point, Sydney, NSW 2061, Australia,
in New Zealand by Random House New Zealand Ltd,
18 Poland Road, Glenfield, Auckland 10, New Zealand
and in South Africa by Random House (Pty) Ltd,
Endulini, 5a Jubilee Road, Parktown 2193, South Africa.

Made and printed in Great Britain by
Cox & Wyman Ltd, Reading, Berkshire

INTRODUCTION

Long ago, the historic county of Medland was made up of four separate regions. These divisions can now only be found on ancient maps, but people living in the old North, South, East and West Quarters remain loyal to their own area.

One example of how the traditional keen rivalry still survives is the County Cup, a season-long soccer tournament for schools. Group games have already been played, and the Quarter Champions are about to clash in the two-legged, semi-final stage of the competition.

The eventual Cup Winners will receive the much-prized silver trophy and earn the right to call themselves the County Champions – the top team in Medland.

THE COUNTY OF MEDLAND

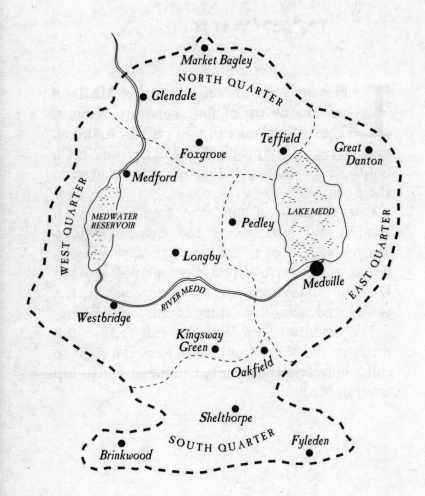

Market Bagley

NORTH QUARTER

Glendale

Teffield

Great
Danton

Foxgrove

WEST QUARTER

Medford

MEDWATER
RESERVOIR

LAKE MEDD

Pedley

Longby

Medville

RIVER MEDD

EAST QUARTER

Westbridge

Kingsway
Green

Oakfield

Shelthorpe

Fyleden

SOUTH QUARTER

Brinkwood

QUARTER CHAMPIONS

From the original sixteen schools that qualified to play in the County Cup this season, these are the Quarter Champions. Check the map to see where the schools are situated.

NORTH QUARTER
Glendale Community School

EAST QUARTER (Joint)
Lakeview High School, Medville

Medville Comprehensive School

SOUTH QUARTER
St Wystan's Comprehensive School, Brinkwood

WEST QUARTER
Westbridge Community College

MEET THE TEAMS

The semi-final knockout stage of the County Cup involves some of the best young footballers in Medland. The players have been eagerly looking forward to the matches ever since the draw was made before the Christmas holidays.

SEMI-FINAL DRAW

SOUTH QUARTER   V   EAST QUARTER
WEST QUARTER   V   NORTH QUARTER

Ties to be played over two legs on 31 January and 28 February

Winners decided on aggregate scores. If goals are level, the tie goes to a play-off, plus extra time and penalties if necessary.

Let's concentrate here on the **South v East semi-final** – although of course we still await the outcome of the play-off between the two big Medville rivals. Meet the teams on the next few pages, replay the highlights of their group action and then enjoy all the excitement of the County Cup.

ST WYSTAN'S COMPREHENSIVE SCHOLL

Medium-sized comprehensive school in the village of Brinkwood in the South Quarter.

Headteacher: *Mr Roy Daniels*
Deputy headteacher: *Mr Ronald Calvert*
P.E. teacher: *Mr Larry Cooper*
School colours: *all-green*
Year 7 soccer captain: *Simon James*
Usual team formation: *4–3–3*

Year 7 soccer squad:

Mark Brown

Josh Rowlands Kushal Bhatia Steve Varley Ben Udal

Stuart O'Leary Lee Melling Michael Earl

(Jag)
Jagdish Hira David Butler Simon James

plus: Graham Nixon, Pete Chambers, Ryan Witchell, Keith Stewart, Eddie Kirk

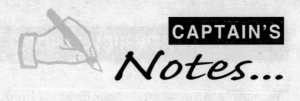

Ever since the start of our County Cup campaign, I've been writing a monthly Captain's Log in the student magazine, Up the Saints! Thought it might just be for a term, but we're still going strong - and let's hope our luck is as well. Holders Shelthorpe messed up their last match so we finished top. We even pinched their coach, Mr Calvert, who jokes that he only came here because he couldn't bear to be parted from the Cup. Mr Cooper will continue in charge of the team, but I wonder what might happen if we lose the first leg at home?

Doubt it. We've got such a good settled side, it's not been easy even for a quality striker like Eddie Kirk to get a regular place. Jag, David and me have been scoring enough goals to keep him on the bench.

We don't know who our semi-final opponents will be yet, and a few of us are planning to go up to Medville and watch the play-off. Whatever the result there, we're all quietly confident that we can keep the County Cup in the South. Mr Calvert might even turn out to be our lucky mascot!

LAKEVIEW HIGH SCHOOL

Medium-sized secondary school in the county town of Medville in the East Quarter. Pupils in year groups 7, 8 and 9 only, aged between 11 and 14.

Headteacher: *Mr John Underwood*
P.E. teacher: *Miss Ruth Jackson*
School colours: *blue shirts, white shorts and socks*
Year 7 soccer captain: *Ben Thorpe*
Usual team formation: *3–5–2, using wing-backs*

Year 7 soccer squad

Michael King (Elvis)

James Black Andy Peacock Harry Glenn

Joe Vernon   Dan Maynard
Steve Jarvis Ben Thorpe Ian Coates
(Henry)
Matthew Tudor Jaspal Singh

plus: Gary (Gordon) Bennett, Manjit Bedi, Will Freeman, Thomas Farr, Alan Davis, Nathan Finch

CAPTAIN'S
Notes...

We've got some unfinished business to see to before we can really think about the semi-final — beating the Comp in the play-off. Miss Jackson, our soccer coach — a pretty good player herself, by the way — has even banned any talk about the semis until we actually get there. And we will, don't worry. It'd be terrible if we let the old enemy from across town knock us out.

Trouble is, the big showdown is away from home as the group game between us took place here. That was the day Harry went missing and everybody thought he'd drowned in Lake Medd. He plays for us now instead — a kind of free transfer from the Comp.

Our main problem, though, is that we lost our leading scorer, Ravi, last term and he's been difficult to replace. Up to the likes of Henry, Jaspal and me, I guess, to get our names on the scoresheet more often in future if we're going to win the County Cup.

MEDVILLE COMPREHENSIVE SCHOOL

L arge comprehensive school in the county town of Medville in the East Quarter.

Headteacher: *Mr Alan Fuller*
P.E. teacher: *Mr Steve Yardley*
School colours: *all-red*
Year 7 soccer captain: *Ryan Burns*
Usual team formation: *4–3–3*

Year 7 soccer squad

Ryan Burns

(Skinny)
Matthew Twigg   Sam Kitson   Afzal Malik   David Ball
(Pram-Man)   (Monty)
Paramjit Maan   Mark Emerson   Jack Montgomery

Robin Yorke   Adam Bridges   Scott Joyner

plus: **Anil Shah, Josh Manchester (United), Satish Gupte, Phil Carter, George Bingham, Aaron Statham**

CAPTAIN'S Notes...

Yo! I'm Ryan Burns, keeper and captain of Medville Comp, last year's runners-up in the County Cup. This season, we're gonna win it!

First things first. Lakeview High were dead lucky to sneak a share of the Quarter title with us, so we've got to play them again to prove who's really the best team in town. No bother. We've already thrashed them at home in the league 4-1.

Then watch out St Wystan's! My mate Monty's already dubbed that match 'Saints v. Sinners'! We're a tough lot, and I don't mind admitting we can be a bit rough too if we have to. We don't take any prisoners. But we can sure play as well. We're after the Treble – League, local cup and County Cup. What a record that will be!

We've got a side packed with Area team players, as I'm sure you know, and getting the ball past me in goal is no easy task. We're winners – so join the Reds if you don't want to end up as losers!

CUP TRAIL

South Quarter

FINAL GROUP TABLE

	P	W	D	L	Goals F	A	(GD)	Pts
St Wystan's	3	2	0	1	7	4	(+3)	6
Shelthorpe	3	2	0	1	7	5	(+2)	6
Oakfield	3	1	0	2	9	8	(+1)	3
Fyleden	3	1	0	2	3	9	(−6)	3

Equal on points, the Saints just pipped the Cup holders Shelthorpe on goal difference to become Quarter Champions.

Group Highlights

... 'This is rubbish!' fumed Matt, the Shelthorpe captain. 'We're supposed to be the County Champions – so let's start playing like it.'

***

... *Matt led by example, chasing, blocking, tackling – and finally scoring. His rising shot clipped the underside of the bar and buried itself in the bottom of the Saints net like an unexploded bomb.*

***

... 'That was our big chance and we've blown it,' sighed the Saints captain, Simon James, after their home defeat by the Cup holders.

***

... *The Shelthorpe players stared at the vandalism in horror. Broken pieces of crossbars littered the penalty areas and some of the wooden posts, snapped in half, leant crookedly in their sockets.*

***

... 'Old Calvert's handed his notice in,' sniggered Jaz, Matt's elder brother. 'Your precious team's losing its coach at Christmas!'

. . . *Captain's Log: The Saints can only pray now that Fyleden will beat Shelthorpe – they say football's a funny old game, but that'd be ridiculous!*

***

. . . 'The County Cup – it's gone! The trophy cabinet's been smashed!'

***

. . . *'I'm asking you one last time, Jaz,' Matt repeated, breathing heavily. 'WHERE'S THE CUP?'*

***

. . . Despairing fingers clawed the ball out of the top corner, but they weren't the goalie's – the hand belonged to the Shelthorpe captain. Penalty!

***

. . . *Matt gazed at the trophy for one last time. 'I know who's really to blame that we lost,' he muttered. 'I'm gonna get Jaz for this.'*

***

. . . Captain's Log: Amazing – the Saints are Quarter Champions! And it's even weirder that Shelthorpe's coach, Mr Calvert, is going to be our new deputy head!

CUP TRAIL

East Quarter

FINAL GROUP TABLE

	P	W	D	L	Goals F	A	(GD)	Pts
Lakeview	3	1	2	0	5	3	(+2)	5
Medville	3	1	2	0	5	3	(+2)	5
Needham College	3	1	0	2	3	6	(−3)	3
Great Danton	3	0	2	1	2	3	(−1)	2

Lakeview and Medville were joint Quarter Champions, dead level on points, goal difference and goals scored.

Group Highlights

. . . Cousin Joe had told him all about Jacko, but this was the first time Harry had seen the Lakeview P.E. teacher. 'Wish she was at the Comp instead of old Yardley,' he grunted.

***

. . . *'You're a traitor, Harry Glenn,' snarled Ryan, the Comp captain. 'You're not fit to be in our squad.'*

***

. . . 'I've got some bad news, miss,' admitted Ravi, Lakeview's leading scorer. 'I'm going to be leaving here soon.'

***

. . . *'Trick or treat, Glenn?' Ryan smirked. 'Let's dunk him in the lake.'*

***

. . . 'Mum's walked out,' Harry confessed to his cousin. 'Told Mum and Dad I wanted to leave the Comp and they had a big row.'

***

. . . *'Typical! You give a boy the chance to play and he can't even be bothered to turn up,' fumed Mr Yardley. 'Glenn had better have some very good excuse or he's had it now.'*

. . . 'Fears are growing for the safety of eleven-year-old Harry Glenn who has gone missing near Lake Medd,' announced the radio news. 'Police frogmen are being called in to help with the search.'

***

. . . *'Just decided to run away,' said Harry. 'I didn't think anybody cared what happened to me.'*

***

. . . 'Why don't you come to the bonfire at Lakeview tonight, Harry, and meet your future teammates?' Joe suggested.

***

. . . *'I could kill Pram-Man for kicking the ball off the line right at the end,' Harry muttered. 'A play-off against the Comp was the last thing I wanted.'*

***

. . . 'Glad it's worked out like this,' Ryan cackled. 'Gives us the chance to prove who's really the best team in town.'

FORM GUIDE

St Wystan's

Placed third in eight-school South Quarter league. Boosted by surprise qualification for County Cup semi-final, the Saints won their last three league games before Christmas without conceding a goal. Still in local cup too.

Leading goalscorers: Butler – 12, Hira – 9
County Cup goalscorers: Hira – 3, James – 2, Butler – 1, Varley – 1

Lakeview

Lying fourth in ten-school East Quarter league table. Drawing too many games they should have won due to lack of goals after losing main striker, Ravi Mistry, in early November. Knocked out of local cup in first round.

Leading goalscorers: Mistry – 8, Tudor – 5
County Cup goalscorers: Mistry – 2, Vernon – 1, Thorpe – 1, Tudor – 1

Medville

Runaway leaders of East Quarter league, having lost only one game before Christmas, and on target for the league and cup double after reaching semi-finals of the local cup competition too.

Leading goalscorers: Bridges – 15, Yorke – 10, Joyner – 8

County Cup goalscorers: Bridges – 2, Yorke – 1, Joyner – 1, Montgomery – 1

. . . Right, you now have all the information you need to make a choice. Which school do you think will eventually reach the County Cup Final? Or perhaps, who do you most want to get through? Read on and find out what happens . . .

FALSE START

. . . scene: Medville Comprehensive School, Saturday morning, 10th January – cousins Joe and Harry are standing in the centre-circle of a frozen football pitch. The big match is off . . .

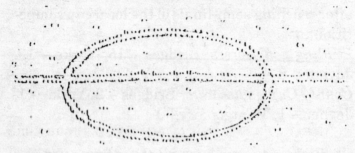

Harry scuffed his left wellie against a solid clump of turf. 'Might have known this would happen,' he sighed. 'I've really had to psych myself up to come back here for the play-off and now I'll have to go through it all over again.'

Joe nodded in understanding. 'Yeah, but you wouldn't have fancied falling on this – it's rock hard. You'd break your arm, dead easy.'

'We had to turn up, though. Old Yardley might have claimed the game or something, otherwise,' Harry muttered, referring to his former P.E.

24

teacher at the Comp. 'Wouldn't put it past him, trying to pull a fast one like that.'

As soon as the match had been officially postponed, their Lakeview teammates drifted away in disappointment, but Harry had persuaded his cousin to hang back for a short while. Reluctant to leave immediately, he stared across the pitch at the school building in which he'd endured such an unhappy time at the start of the previous term.

'C'mon, Harry, I thought you'd have seen enough of this place,' Joe moaned, shivering. 'Let's go home. I'm freezing.'

'Soz, it's just that it brings back so many bad memories.'

'So why are you wanting to stick around longer than you have to?'

Harry gave a shrug. 'Oh, I dunno. Guess I was hoping it might help to lay a few ghosts, y'know, if I could now view the Comp for what it really is – just another school to come and play football at.'

'Well, if you can't, don't go and do a runner again in these temperatures,' Joe grinned. 'You'd probably end up like a big icicle.'

Harry suddenly let out a low groan. 'That's all I need!'

Joe glanced towards the school and recognized the three figures who were swaggering towards them. They weren't only ghosts from Harry's past. Joe had also had a few confrontations himself with Ryan, Adam and Monty.

'Somehow, I don't reckon they're coming over to wish us a Happy New Year, do you?' he said.

Joe was right. Ryan's greeting was far from friendly.

'Didn't expect to find you pair of losers still here,' the Comp captain called out. 'What you up to?'

Joe rose to the challenge. 'Just thinking how lucky Harry was to get away from a dump like this,' he retorted.

'Harry? Who's Harry?' sneered Monty, continuing their usual baiting of his cousin. 'There's only this wimp Glenn here.'

'They must all be wimps at Lakeview,' put in Adam. 'Cried off from playing the match just 'cos of a bit of frost. Scared they might fall down and hurt their knees, poor little diddums!'

As the trio burst into cackles, Harry saw Joe's fists clenching and put a restraining hand on his arm. 'Save it, Joe, they're not worth it,' he hissed.

It was too late. Joe wasn't in the mood to take any kind of cheek. 'Don't try and blame us,' he

26

said angrily. 'The pitch isn't fit and you know it.'

'Rubbish!' Ryan snapped. 'Would've thawed out as the match went on. We'd already got changed.'

'Just shows how stupid you lot are, then.'

They might well have come to blows at that point if a loud voice hadn't put an abrupt end to the argument. It belonged to Mr Yardley.

'Oi! Let's have all you lads home,' bellowed the teacher from the car park. 'I want to lock these gates.'

Ryan held Joe's scornful glare for several seconds longer and then broke the tension, turning away. 'C'mon, you guys,' he said to his mates. 'This can wait – that's if these two dare show their faces again next week.'

'And if they do, I'll make sure they both get a good gobful of my boots,' snarled Monty. 'They're gonna get the full treatment.'

Adam sniggered. 'Right – the full Monty!'

. . . sounds like there will be more than local pride at stake when the Medville schools rearrange the Cup showdown – the cousins keeping a full set of teeth for a start . . .

MEDVILLE v LAKEVIEW

Saturday 17 January
k.o. 10 a.m.
Referee: Mr F. O'Donald

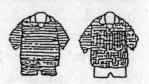

... a rise in temperature allows the long-awaited play-off to go ahead at last, but tempers are soon heating up too – the neutral referee will need to keep a firm grip on the game ...

'Come here, number six, I want a word with you.'

Jack Montgomery was the picture of innocence. 'Me, ref?'

'Yes, you. You had no intention of playing that ball. You just ploughed straight into that lad.'

Monty was having to work hard to prevent a smirk spreading across his face and ruining his act. 'Accidental collision, ref.'

'Nonsense, boy. It was a deliberate crude foul.'

Mr O'Donald glanced at his watch, thinking he must have awarded more free-kicks in the first quarter of an hour than he normally did in a whole match. The Needham College teacher had been caught unawares by the intensity of the local Derby. While Miss Jackson was on the pitch, attending to the injured player, he called the two captains together.

'Tell your players to calm down,' he insisted. 'They only seem interested in kicking lumps out of each other.'

'They started it,' Ryan claimed. 'Their number two fouled our winger.'

'Rubbish! He tripped Joe first,' countered Ben.

The referee shut them up. 'The game's not worth playing if it's going to carry on like this. I've a good mind to abandon it and have both schools disqualified.'

'What, so your own College team can take part in the semis instead?' Ryan snorted.

Mr O'Donald realized that it was a threat he shouldn't have made. 'Don't say you haven't been warned, captains, that's all,' he sighed. 'I don't want to have to start sending people off.'

He went to check on the injury and Miss Jackson showed him the gash on Harry's leg. 'I'll need to bring on a sub,' she said. 'The cut's too deep for him to play on.'

Adam Bridges sniggered as he saw Harry limping off the pitch. 'Well done, Monty. One down, one to go.'

'I'll get that Joe too,' Monty promised. 'Just waiting for the right moment – and I'll make sure the ref doesn't see me next time.'

There were few neutrals among the large crowd of partisan spectators, but four of them were taking a very keen interest in everything that had been happening. They had made the journey up to Medville from the village of Brinkwood in the South Quarter especially to see the game.

'A right load of bruisers we've got here, Simon,' muttered Mr James. 'I reckon you'll all need to wear two pairs of shinpads in the semis.'

'We'll be OK, Dad,' said the Saints' captain, exchanging grins with his teammates who had come to help spy out the opposition. 'We can look after ourselves.'

'Better tell Cooper what they're like, though, so he doesn't forget his red card,' said David Butler, the Saints' leading scorer.

'Yeah, if he sends a few of them off in the first leg, we'll win easy,' laughed Steve Varley, who played in central defence.

'Surprised your teacher didn't come to watch this play-off himself,' said Mr James. 'He might have spotted some weaknesses.'

'You could have brought your camcorder and let Cooper study the match video,' suggested Steve cheekily, slipping Simon a wink. He knew that was still a touchy subject after Mr James had missed his son's goal when he filmed their last group match.

'Perhaps a good job I didn't, eh? A dirty match like this might have needed an X-certificate! Too much violence to show to kids your age.'

'It's kids our age doing it,' David pointed out.

Apart from the odd wild challenge, the players were now exercising a greater degree of self-control in case the referee decided to make an example of them. The standard of football had distinctly improved as a result.

Lakeview gradually gained the upper hand before half-time, forcing the home side on to the defensive with a spell of sustained pressure.

Wing-backs Joe and Dan were joining in the attacks to good effect, but no-one could find a way past the garishly yellow-clad Ryan in the Comp goal.

Even the Saints on the touchline applauded his brilliant double save when it seemed that Lakeview simply had to score. Ryan thwarted both the Blue strikers in the space of a few seconds, first by blocking Henry's near-post header and then scrambling across his line in time to push Jaspal's rebound effort round the opposite post.

'That keeper's gonna take some beating if we play the Comp,' said David in grudging admiration.

Simon nodded. 'Maybe it won't be our problem. The Blues are well on top now. They might yet do the job for us.'

Lakeview had to wait until first-half stoppage time before they proved that it could be done, and Ben's skill made the art of scoring look deceptively easy. The captain's instant control of a firmly-hit pass gave him all the time he needed to look up, choose his spot and then steer the ball with the inside of his right foot wide of the keeper's dive. The shot was all about accuracy, not power, and Ryan could get nowhere near it.

. . . so Lakeview have their noses in front at half-time, just 1–0 ahead, but in such a tight, hard-fought game, it's a precious lead – don't miss the second half to see whether they will be able to hold on to it . . .

SECOND HALF

. . . let's eavesdrop on both camps at half-time to hear what's being said . . .

'You know the way I want you to play, boys. What is it?'

'Hard but fair, miss,' chorused the Lakeview players sheepishly. It was a maxim that Miss Jackson had drummed into them the previous term.

'Right – hard but fair,' she repeated. 'Keep playing football in the right spirit, that's the important thing at your age, whatever the provocation.'

'But it's difficult not to retaliate, miss, when somebody tries to maim one of your teammates,' said Joe. 'We can't just let them get away with it.'

'No, but what's the use of getting yourself sent off? The best way to hit back is to knock them out the Cup. We might do it with eleven men, but not ten.'

Thirty metres away, Mr Yardley was putting

a similar message across to the Comp players in his own style. He tossed the match ball firmly into Monty's arms.

'What's this for?' said Monty, startled.

'You might well ask,' Mr Yardley retorted. 'I'm not surprised you don't seem to know. This round thing's called a football, but it's been a waste of time having it on the pitch first half. Some of you have been too busy with your own private feuds to bother playing with it.'

The boys hung their heads, staring at the ground, not wanting to accept their share of the blame. Only Ryan was bold enough to speak up.

'This ref's got it in for us. We've only got to touch one of their players and he gives a free-kick.'

'Depends what you mean by *touch*,' the teacher said sourly. 'The way Monty bulldozed into Glenn was hardly a welcome back gesture to a former teammate, was it?'

'Actually, it's Harry, Mr Yardley,' put in Paramjit quietly.

'What is? I mean, who is?' he stammered, taken aback by the midfielder's interruption.

'Harry Glenn, Mr Yardley. You always called him by his surname. That's why everybody started teasing him over it.'

'I thought Glenn was his first name.'

'Drop it, Pram-Man,' said Adam. 'You don't have to stick up for him just 'cos you went to the same primary school.'

'Forget about Glenn,' Ryan snarled. 'What matters now is that we're losing. So let's get back out there, guys, and stuff them this half.'

As the teams lined up, Mr Yardley wandered over to the injured boy. Harry saw him coming and pretended to be engrossed in retying his bootlace.

'Er . . . sorry about your leg . . . er . . . Harry,' he stumbled. 'How bad is it?'

Harry could hardly believe his ears. Not only was it the first time he'd ever heard Mr Yardley apologize, but also because he hadn't been called Glenn. He almost forgot to answer the question.

'A bit sore, but don't reckon it will need stitches or anything,' he managed to say.

'Glad to hear that. I'm sure old Monty didn't mean to hurt you.'

Harry didn't reply at all this time.

'Right, well, I hope things are working out better for you at the High School,' said the P.E. teacher to cover his embarrassment before moving away to watch the game again.

'Trying his best to be human, I suppose,' Harry

muttered under his breath. 'Better late than never.'

Mr Yardley was soon to be seen behaving more like a trained chimp, scampering along the touchline in delight as if he'd just been offered a bunch of bananas. The Comp had equalized in their very first attack, Adam sweeping the ball into the net from a right-wing cross.

Five minutes later, the number nine scored again. Or at least he thought so. His fierce strike from just inside the penalty area had flashed past the goalie's groping hand, but the ball smacked against the underside of the crossbar, ricocheted to the ground at a steep angle and bounced away out of danger.

GOAL!

Adam was well into his goal-celebration dance routine when he realized no-one else was joining in. The referee had waved play-on.

'That was in, ref!' he wailed.

'Sorry – no goal. The whole ball must cross the line.'

'You've got to be joking!'

'Don't argue, lad,' said Mr O'Donald. 'Get on with the game.'

Loud protests could be heard from the Comp supporters, most of them with only distant views of the controversial incident. Their shouts resounded over the school playing fields.

'Goal, referee! You want to borrow my specs?'

'Go and consult your guide dog, ref!'

'I don't believe it,' choked Mr Yardley. 'He's not giving it.'

Adam's teammates were just as adamant that it was a goal.

'The ball was well over the line,' the left-winger complained. 'I was the nearest one to it.'

Ryan even ran up as far as the centre-circle to add his voice to the angry debate. 'C'mon, ref,' the captain shouted. 'Certain goal, that.'

NO GOAL

BLUES' VIEW

The spectators on the opposite touchline were equally vociferous in support of the referee.

'Good decision, ref. Spot on!'

'No way that ball crossed the line.'

'You have to give the benefit of the doubt to the defenders in a situation like that,' said Ben's father.

Harry was standing next to his teacher about level with the edge of the Blues' penalty area. 'What do you think, miss?' he asked.

Miss Jackson shook her head. 'Can't really tell from this angle, can we? Just have to count it as a lucky let off. We could easily have been 2–1 down now.'

'Elvis didn't reckon it went in,' said Harry as the Lakeview goalkeeper shooed his players upfield. 'He was ready to save any rebound.'

'I don't think he knew what happened,' she grinned. 'Anyway, there's only one person whose opinion matters in the end.'

'Who's that, miss?' he said, half-guessing the answer.

'The referee. He's always right, remember – even if he's wrong!'

Mr O'Donald had tried, as best he could, to ignore all the comments – both for and against. He knew the two sets of supporters were seeing the game through biased eyes. But as he jogged towards the halfway line there was one accusation that was too much to take. It came from one of the players running after him.

'You're a cheat, referee!'

Mr O'Donald glanced round to try and identify the culprit and then blew his whistle to halt play. He strode up to the boy. 'Would you mind repeating what you've just called me?' he demanded fiercely.

Monty sagged visibly, not expecting the referee to turn on him. He knew he was in deep trouble.

'Well? Speak up. Now's your chance.'

Monty remained silent.

'Right, despite what some people think, my eyes are working very well – and so are my ears. You're off!'

'You're sending me off?' Monty gasped. 'You can't do that.'

'Wrong again. You've gone too far this time. Go on – off!'

It was a long, lonely walk. Monty didn't dare to catch Mr Yardley's eye and kept on walking towards the changing room. His County Cup was over.

And so it was, ultimately, for the rest of his teammates, who were stunned by Monty's dismissal. For a while, the game continued without him in an almost unreal atmosphere of anti-climax, but it burst into life again when Lakeview's number ten, Jaspal Singh, fastened on to a through ball from Ben and fired his shot low past Ryan's sprawling dive.

'Magic, Jaspal!' cried Ben. 'Hit a few more like that and perhaps we won't miss Ravi as much as we thought.'

The double handicap of being a man short and a goal behind proved too much for the Reds to overcome. In fact, if Henry hadn't pumped another good chance over the crossbar, the visitors might well have won the play-off by a more comfortable margin.

When the referee blew the final whistle, only Miss Jackson went up to shake his hand. Mr Yardley deliberately kept his distance. He didn't trust himself not to say something that he might later regret. He felt that far too much had been said already.

Result:	Medville 1 v 2 Lakeview	
	h-t: 0 –1	
Scorers:	Bridges	Thorpe, Singh

Man of the Match: **Jaspal Singh**

FLOODLIGHT FOCUS

. . . on **Jaspal Singh**

school	Lakeview High
other teams	none
position	striker
best foot forward	left-footed
age	11
build	tall and thin
ambition	to become a doctor
pets	none
family	one older brother, two younger sisters
superstitions	always put my left boot on first
hobbies	computer games, collecting stickers
so embarrassing!	once kicked flagpost when taking a corner
favourites	
school subject	science
football team	Oxford United
book	BFG by Roald Dahl
TV programme	The Simpsons
music	rap
food/drink	pizza, coke
word/saying	cool

TUNING UP

. . . on the following Saturday, the Saints are in action for the first time in the New Year – let's just catch the end of their league match . . .

'Great shot, Dave!' Simon yelled in the scorer's ear as they celebrated the goal that clinched the three points. 'Hope you've got your shooting boots on again next week in the Cup.'

David Butler grinned at his captain. 'You can clean them for me if you like.'

'No way! Just make sure they're still in good working order.'

'You bet. Can't wait to show Lakeview what they can do.'

David had bagged both the goals in the 2–0 victory and there was barely time for the match to restart before Mr Cooper blew the final whistle.

'Well played, lads,' he praised them as they gathered briefly around their coach. 'The team-work was pretty good once you'd scraped off the holiday rust. I'm sure Mr Calvert's been impressed with what he's seen.'

The players hadn't realized that their new deputy headteacher had been watching the action from an upstairs window of the school. They glanced at one another, each privately hoping to have caught the eye of the man who'd won the County Cup last season with his own team at Shelthorpe.

'Do away goals count double in the Cup, Mr Cooper?' asked David. 'Y'know, like in Europe?'

The teacher smiled. 'No, fortunately, we don't want to stretch your maths too much. Just simple adding up will do. We need to score more than them over the two legs, that's all.'

Five minutes later, the boys' changing room was a noisy, steam-filled place with goalkeeper Mark Brown especially exuberant. 'Magic! My fourth clean sheet on the trot,' he cried as he paddled out of the showers.

'More than can be said for your towel,' said David. 'It's filthy. You're supposed to use it after you've got all the mud off, you know, not before.'

'Us defenders might take some of the credit, not just you,' laughed Steve, flicking his own towel at the goalkeeper's bare backside. 'I don't know how you got so muddy. You hardly had anything to do this morning.'

'What about my brilliant save when you let that kid stroll past you?'

'Brilliant? You could have bent down to pick the ball up. You didn't have to do such a spectacular dive.'

'He just likes rolling about in puddles,' laughed David. 'Mark's not happy unless he's covered in mud.'

The joking continued as the boys dried themselves off and started to get dressed, but then their thoughts turned to more serious business.

'What were Lakeview really like?' Mark asked. 'Are they much cop?'

'Good enough to stain your precious sheet if we're not careful,' said Steve. 'They put two past a real goalkeeper.'

Mark pulled a face. 'Ha, ha, very funny!'

'I'm not saying Lakeview didn't deserve to win, but that disallowed goal was the turning point of the match,' said Simon. 'If the ref had given it, we might have been playing the Comp instead.'

'Glad we're not,' said David, examining two new bruises on his legs. 'Might have collected a lot more of these, the way some of their guys tackled.'

The captain shrugged. 'Anyway, doesn't matter now. The semi was always going to be

tough, whoever got through,' he pointed out. 'There aren't any easy matches at this stage of the County Cup. The teams left in are all Quarter Champions – just like us.'

That was enough to spark off the Saints' favourite chant and soon everybody was joining in, their raucous voices echoing off the tiles. 'Champions! Champions! Champions!'

BE PREPARED

. . . Meanwhile, over at Lakeview, Miss Jackson has been listening carefully to the weather forecasts . . .

'I'm choosing the same side as for the play-off,' Miss Jackson announced at the squad's midweek training session. 'No reason to change a winning team.'

Eleven boys were delighted at that news. The others had to try and conceal their disappointment and hope their chance might come in the second leg at home in a month's time.

Harry had already declared himself fit again and would play on the left of the back three in the Blues' 3–5–2 formation. He had made that position his own since transferring to Lakeview half way through last term.

'If we can get a draw on Saturday, I reckon we'll be good enough to go through over the two legs on aggregate,' he said to his cousin as they warmed up for a four-a-side practice game.

'We're not going there just to play for a draw,' Joe insisted. 'We're gonna win.'

Their team won the short, hectic game that followed too. The players were only allowed two touches in possession, but often they only needed one. The winning goal was the result of a swift exchange of passes between the cousins, which ended with Joe sliding the ball home.

Miss Jackson was well pleased. 'Good skills, you two,' she called out. 'I couldn't have done that better myself.'

The boys grinned, although they knew that she probably could do it just as well. They'd seen Ruth Jackson play wing-back for Medville Ladies and had read in the local paper that she'd scored in a recent inter-county match for Medland. Their coach didn't need anybody else to show how something should be done. She was perfectly capable of demonstrating the technique herself.

'I'm afraid colder weather is being forecast again for the weekend,' she warned the players before they went back into school for a late lunch. 'I don't think it's going to snow, but it's likely to be frosty overnight.'

'Oh, no!' Ben exclaimed. 'The game won't be postponed, will it?'

'I hope not, but the ground might be too hard to take a stud. Have your trainers with you as well as boots to test which give you better grip,' she advised. 'You won't be much use to the team if you're falling over every time you try and turn. Good footballers need to be prepared to play in all kinds of conditions.'

. . . before the first leg clash at Brinkwood, it might be an idea to check out what the County Coach has to say about different formations . . .

COUNTY COACH

FORMATIONS

There are many different team formations, but it's important for a coach to choose a system that suits the players available, not vice versa. A better-organized team can often beat more talented opposition.

✓ Formations need flexibility, allowing players to adapt during a game

✓ Formation patterns start from the back, not counting the goalkeeper

✓ Formations like 4–4–2 are more defensive than 4–3–3 or 4–2–4

✓ A 3–5–2 system has three main defenders, with wing-backs in support

✓ A defensive sweeper system often lines up as 1–4–3–2 or 4–1–3–2

✓ A team outnumbering the opposition in midfield can dominate a match

✓ Using two wingers in an attacking 4–2–4 system gives a team good width, but can leave it vulnerable in midfield

✓ A 4–3–1–2 system has someone playing 'in the hole' behind the two strikers

✓ You could even play a 4–3–2–1 formation, shaped like a Christmas tree!

LINE UP!

SEMI-FINAL: FIRST LEG

ST WYSTAN'S v LAKEVIEW

Saturday 31 January
k.o. 11 a.m.
Referee: Mr R. Calvert

. . . no snow fortunately, but it's a very cold morning with an icy wind – gloves and trainers are worn by almost all the players, with the goal-keepers also in tracksuit bottoms for extra protection in the bone-hard goalmouths . . .

The fact that the score remained 0–0 at half-time was due partly to the difficult conditions, but mostly to the outstanding form of the two goalkeepers.

During the team talk from Mr Cooper, the Saints' number nine was still muttering to himself and shaking his head in disbelief at how Elvis had saved his point-blank range shot just before the interval.

'Are you listening to me, David?' said the teacher suddenly.

'Er, yes, Mr Cooper.'

'So what have you got to say?'

'Um . . .'

His teammates sniggered as David's face flushed. He clearly had no idea what Mr Cooper had been talking about.

'I was wanting to know why you're getting caught offside so often,' he repeated.

David shrugged. 'Can't help it. I thought the ref was supposed to be on our side.'

'Don't try and blame Mr Calvert. He isn't on anybody's side while he's reffing, you know that.'

As if to emphasize his neutrality, Mr Calvert was standing on his own in the centre-circle, resisting his natural impulses to go across and speak to the players. As a coach, there were several things that he would have liked to change – but as the referee, he didn't feel in a position to do so.

'Not my team,' he reminded himself. 'I wouldn't like it now if some new bloke came and started trying to interfere with how I run things.'

Mr Calvert blew the whistle for the teams to line up for the second half and took the chance to have a quick word with the captain. 'Any substitutions?' he asked.

Simon shook his head. 'No, but I think Mr Cooper might have wished he could have made about ten. Not playing very well, are we?'

'More a case that Lakeview aren't letting you. They've had a stranglehold on the game so far, especially in midfield.'

'What can we do about it?'

'Easier said than done, but you need to get at their back three quicker. By the time the ball gets through to them, they're stepping up and playing people offside. I expect Mr Cooper's already mentioned that.'

'Sort of,' Simon sighed.

The second half began to follow much the same pattern as the first, with the Saints' skilful midfield trio being given very little room to manoeuvre. The Blues' wing-backs, Joe and Dan, pushed forward into that vital area at every opportunity to outnumber the green shirts five to three.

Just when the game had drifted into near-stalemate, Simon wriggled past Joe's challenge and then switched play with a cross-field, diagonal pass. Right-winger Jagdish found himself with more space than he'd had all match. He enjoyed it so much that he tried to hold on to possession for too long, allowing Harry to make a well-timed tackle and rob him of the ball.

Harry carried the ball upfield some distance before Ben took over and the captain unleashed a shot at goal from the edge of the penalty area. Only a soaring save from Mark, leaping high to his right, kept the scoreline blank.

It didn't stay that way for much longer. Within the next five minutes, the ball was in the net at both ends of the pitch – but only one goal counted.

The Saints 'scored' first. Simon again was the provider, curling a left-footed centre into the danger area for David Butler to smash the ball home. The striker was so excited 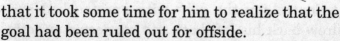 that it took some time for him to realize that the goal had been ruled out for offside.

David was devastated. 'No way was I offside then,' he protested.

Mr Calvert gave the boy a stern look. 'Not you, the winger,' he explained, excusing David his heat-of-the-moment outburst.

Jagdish joined in, trying to make his complaint sound more respectful. 'I wasn't interfering with play, sir,' he began. 'I was just following up in case there was a rebound.'

'Sorry, lads, that's not how I saw it. When David shot, you were well offside, Jagdish. And in my view, you were distracting the goalkeeper.'

The boys realized there was no sense in arguing further. Mr Calvert was clearly not going to change his mind.

While the Saints were still ruing their misfortune, the visitors forced two successive corners on the left. After hitting the first across high and long, Dan screwed the second one back unexpectedly to a teammate lurking in space just outside the area. Harry had wandered further forward than intended, having no-one to mark temporarily as the Saints had left only David upfield. Two other defenders were looking after him.

Controlling the pass with one touch, Harry drew back his left boot and connected sweetly, driving the ball low through a mass of bodies in the crowded penalty box. Several other feet tried in vain to make contact and Mark barely saw the ball until it was too late. By the time he dived, it was nestling behind him, mocking his efforts.

It was the first goal that Harry had ever scored in a proper match – and it proved to be the decider.

'We're not out of it yet,' Simon said defiantly as the Saints trudged back to the changing room after the final whistle. 'If they can come and win here, there's no reason why we can't do the same up at their place next month.'

'Well, beating Lakeview is going to be easy compared to what you've got to do now,' David muttered.

'What's that?' asked Simon, puzzled.

'Write your next *Captain's Log* piece for the mag without blaming Calvert for costing us the match!'

Result:	St. Wystan's 0 v 1 Lakeview
	h-t: 0 – 0
Scorers:	Glenn
Men of the Match: **Mark Brown and Michael King**	

. . . it's the turn of two goalkeepers this time to share the glare of the Cup floodlights . . .

FLOODLIGHT FOCUS

. . . on **Mark Brown**

school	St Wystan's
other teams	South Quarter Area side
	Brinkwood Boys (Sunday League)
position	goalkeeper
best foot forward	right-footed
age	12 years 4 months
build	tall, handsome and athletic!
nickname	none that I know of
ambition	to keep clean sheets
pets	collie dog and goldfish
family	two older sisters
superstitions	always jump up and touch bar before kick-off
hobbies	computers, taking things to pieces
so embarrassing!	letting a goal in through my legs on Saints debut

favourites

school subject	technology
football team	Spurs
book	Clockwork by Philip Pullman
TV programme	any scientific programme
music	pop
food	ice-cream
drink	coke
word/saying	well weird

FLOODLIGHT FOCUS

... on **Michael King**

school	Lakeview high
other teams	Medville Majors (Sunday League)
position	goalie
best foot forward	right-footed
age	12 years 1 month
build	average height, stocky (not fat!)
nickname	Elvis (after the King, Elvis Presley)
ambition	to sing like Elvis!
pets	2 dogs, three cats and a gerbil
family	one older sister, one younger brother
superstitions	none — don't need any good-luck charms!
hobbies	playing or reading about sport
so embarrassing!	it's always dead embarrassing to dive the wrong way trying to save a penalty!

favourites

school subject	Games
football team	Arsenal — the Gunners are dead good!
book	any football stories
TV programme	Neighbours
music	Elvis Presley songs (only joking!)
food	Chinese
drink	coffee (swig of beer when no-one's looking!)
word/saying	dead

UP THE SAINTS!

Captain's Log – Sunday, 1st February

Still brooding after our defeat yesterday in the first leg of the County Cup semi-final. We lost 1-0 at home to Lakeview, the East Champions, so we now face a tough task in the return leg up at Medville. We've only really got ourselves to blame – well, almost – but it wasn't easy to play good football on the bumpy, frosty pitch.

We also seem to have run out of the kind of luck that helped us to reach this stage. Lakeview had it instead, especially when David Butler had a great goal disallowed for offside shortly before they scored the winner. Sadly, Mr Calvert didn't turn out to be our lucky mascot after all.

Defences were on top for most of the game and both goal-keepers were brilliant. Mark Brown shared the honour of Man of the Match with their keeper called Elvis and both of them pulled off some incredible saves. Elvis lives!

We've not given up hope yet of making the Final of course. With only one goal in it, we've still got a decent chance of winning overall on aggregate. I guess we'll just have to do things the hard way again by winning away like we did twice in the group.

All for now – signing off till next time.

Simon James, 7C

SOUTH v EAST

Saturday 7 February
k.o. 11 a.m.
Referee: L. Cooper

. . . a week later, some of the Cup players are destined to meet again in an Area match, even though the two goalkeeping heroes can only find a place among the subs for their respective Quarters . . .

'OK, lads, East have turned up at last,' announced the South's team manager. 'Let's have you out on the pitch to warm up.'

'Need to as well in this weather,' muttered Steve Varley, the big Saints defender. 'It's freezing.'

'What do you expect?' said Simon. 'It *is* the middle of winter.'

The game was being staged at Shelthorpe Comprehensive and the boys trooped outside just as their opponents were approaching the school building from the car park.

'How many of the Lakeview mob can you spot?' asked Steve.

Simon shrugged. 'Dunno, two or three, maybe. I recognize Ben, their captain. Chance for us to get a bit of revenge on them today, I hope.'

Even Simon didn't anticipate how quickly the South would strike the first blow. Three minutes into the match, they were 1–0 up and his only regret was that the goalkeeper picking the ball out of the net was not Elvis.

'I don't believe it!' Ryan Burns screamed at his defenders. 'You all stood there like shop dummies, giving that kid a free header.'

Nobody cared to look the East captain in the face and accept responsibility for leaving the scorer unmarked. And they also tried to close their ears to the added abuse being bellowed at them from Mr Yardley on the touchline. The Medville teacher wasn't used to seeing his Quarter side defend so sloppily.

Simon caught Ben's eye and chalked up an imaginary figure in the air to let him know the score. Having provided the cross for the opening goal, it was Simon himself who notched number two shortly after the half-time break.

The South captain, Matt Eales of Shelthorpe, burst through from midfield before slipping the ball inside the full-back to send the winger on a clear run for goal. Ryan dashed out to narrow the shooting angle and even attempted to bring him down, but Simon leapt over his flailing arms and had the undiluted pleasure of slamming the ball into the gaping, unguarded net.

With a 2–0 cushion, the South manager made a couple of substitutions, giving Mark Brown a taste of the action for the last quarter of an hour. Lakeview's Henry Tudor welcomed the new goalkeeper immediately with a snap-shot on the turn. Mark had little chance to sight the ball, but his reflexes were sharp enough to allow him time to spring to his left and fingertip it around the post.

Mark wasn't seriously troubled again and South's well-deserved victory meant that they leapfrogged East into second place in the Area league table behind the West Quarter.

Ben made a point of shaking hands with his rival Cup captain as they walked off the pitch. 'See you again after half-term,' he grinned.

Before Simon could respond, they were pounced on from behind by Matt Eales. 'C'mon, you two, I want to show you something,' he laughed.

Half-guessing what it might be, they ripped off their boots and followed Matt along a corridor. 'There you are!' he exclaimed, stopping in front of a large glass cabinet in the school foyer. 'Just feast your eyes on that beauty. It may be the only time one of you will ever see it.'

Simon and Ben gazed in awe at the centre-piece of Shelthorpe's packed trophy cabinet – the gleaming silver County Cup!

'Wow! It's massive!' breathed Ben. 'I'd love to get my hands on that.'

'Soz, Ben, it's ours,' Simon told him. 'We've got somebody at St Wystan's who's already got a claim on the Cup. He won it last year.'

'Who's that, then?'

Matt answered. 'Our old teacher, Calvert,' he said. 'I don't really care who wins the Cup now that we can't, but I guess it'd be nice for Calvert to keep it for another year.'

'Wasn't he the bloke who disallowed that goal of yours?' cackled Ben, glancing at Simon. 'He can't want to keep the Cup that much.'

'Just one of them things,' Simon grunted, pulling a face. 'Doesn't matter, anyway. He knows we play better away from home.'

Ben smirked. 'Any chance of him reffing the second leg for us as well?'

. . . do you sometimes feel that half-term will never come? Well, just turn over and the holiday's here . . .

KICKABOUT

*. . . scene: Medville Park – a group of Lakeview
lads are enjoying a half-term kickabout until a
couple of uninvited guests crash the party . . .*

'Oh, heck! Look who's coming.'
Harry Glenn's cry of dismay was
genuine. The sight of two of his former
tormentors totally ruined his happy holiday
mood.

'It's OK,' said Ben. 'It's only Ryan and Monty.'

'Only!' exclaimed Joe. 'You mean *only* the guys
who threatened to kick our teeth in.'

'Yeah, and tried to cripple me,' Harry added.
'I'm going home if you let them join in. I don't
want to give Monty a chance to finish the job off,
thanks.'

'Don't be daft. If you clear off now, they'll think
you're a cry-baby,' put in Elvis. 'Besides, their
ball looks better than ours. This is dead light.'

'Yo!' Ryan called out as he and Monty
approached. 'You lot fancy a game?'

'Huh! Typical Ryan, that is,' Harry hissed.
'Acting as if he owns the place. Asks if *we* want
to play with him, not the other way round.'

Joe shrugged. 'Let it rest. You're never gonna change him. Just make it seem as if you're not bothered.'

'All right,' Harry sighed. 'Might as well stay, I suppose. Got nothing else to do, anyway.'

Monty started on him straight away. 'Hey! It's little Glenn, the match-winner!' he scoffed. 'Saints must be pretty bad, if they let *you* score a goal. We'd have slaughtered 'em.'

'Yeah, but you're not in the Cup any more, are you?' Harry pointed out. 'What was the score in that play-off? Two—one, was it?'

'Ancient history,' said Ryan quickly before his pal could react to the taunt. 'Monty wouldn't even have been playing in the semi, anyway. Yardley banned him for a month after that sending-off business.'

Monty beamed like a loon, seemingly proud of the boost the suspension had given to his bad-boy reputation. 'Serves Yardley right. Both the Comp and the Quarter have lost since then 'cos I wasn't playing.'

Elvis butted in. 'Look, are we gonna have a game of footie or stand around gassing all day? How about Lakeview stick the Comp?'

'Er, I know my maths ain't that good, but I make that four against two,' said Joe.

'No, three each. Fancy going on loan back to the Comp, Harry?'

Harry saw Ryan's face fall at the prospect and that helped him to decide. 'Why not?' he grinned. 'At least that might stop Monty kicking me again if I'm on his side.'

'Don't count on it,' Monty muttered under his breath.

'Drop-back goalies, OK?' said Ryan.

'Sure,' Elvis agreed. 'You may be the Area keeper, but I'm better than you out on the pitch.'

To prove his point, Elvis knocked the football out of Monty's hands and kicked it into the goal. 'See!' he laughed. 'We're one–nil up already.'

'Idiot!' Ryan snarled. 'We haven't even decided which way we're kicking yet. Think we'll count that as an own goal.'

The rival banter ensured that there would be a keen, competitive edge to the contest. Everybody knew it wouldn't just be a leisurely, friendly kickabout.

The boys put down coats as goalposts and played across half the football pitch. They charged madly around for the next twenty minutes, burning up their surplus holiday energy, with goals plentiful at either end. The actual score was a matter of some dispute, especially when arguing whether a shot went over or under an imaginary crossbar.

The game ended abruptly. As Ryan crossed the ball too near to Elvis, Monty clattered into the Lakeview goalkeeper as he gathered it safely up into his arms.

'Foul!' Joe cried as Elvis writhed on the grass. 'Watch it, Monty. There was no need to go in so hard.'

'Fifty-fifty ball,' he claimed.

Elvis was now curled up into a ball himself, holding his right arm. 'He's knackered my shoulder,' he swore in pain.

'We've got the second leg of the semis next week and you've just gone and crocked our keeper,' Joe complained bitterly.

'Not my fault he was too slow to get out of the way,' retorted Monty. 'A little tap on the shoulder, that's all it was.'

Elvis was sitting up now, his arm held painfully across his chest as if in a sling. '*A little tap!* You hit me like a runaway tank.'

'C'mon, Monty, time to go,' said Ryan. 'They're all gonna burst into tears soon and the pitch'll get waterlogged.'

'Yeah, see you losers again next week,' chortled Monty. 'The Comp's not got a game then, so we're all gonna come and have a laugh at you lot getting knocked out the Cup.'

'Don't bother,' snapped Ben. 'You'll have a wasted journey. We're going to win it this year.'

Ryan and Monty went off, cackling, to collect their coats, leaving the Lakeview players to consider the gloomy consequences of Elvis's injury.

'I wouldn't put it past them two to have planned something like this,' Harry sighed. 'I know what they're like. Bet they were out to get one of us.'

'And trust it to be Elvis,' muttered Joe. 'Who's gonna play in goal now if he can't?'

There were a number of other players in the squad who often fancied themselves as goalies in practice sessions, but only one name came to Ben's mind as a serious candidate. And that was one who didn't exactly fill the captain with the greatest of confidence.

'Gordon Bennett!' he groaned.

GOOD NEWS, BAD NEWS

. . . the view of the lake from the school playing fields is obscured by rain, but Miss Jackson is still putting her squad through their paces . . .

'Get down quick to those low shots, Gordon,' Elvis called to the goalkeeper. 'The ball might skid about on Saturday if this rain keeps up, so you'll have to make sure you get your body right behind it.'

Gary Bennett, Gordon to his mates, wasn't sure whether to be thrilled or terrified by his sudden, unexpected promotion to the side for the Cup semi-final. He had only played in a couple of friendlies for the school, and neither of those had been particularly happy occasions. Letting one goal in through his legs had been his most embarrassing moment.

Elvis was relieved that Miss Jackson seemed to have taken the news of his injury surprisingly well when he told her about it.

'There's nothing broken, but the shoulder's all bruised and sore,' he reported. 'I can't even raise my arm high enough to scratch my head, see.'

He dragged his right arm out of its supportive sling and tried to demonstrate, but he could barely even scratch his chin without wincing. 'Doctor said I've got to rest it for a while,' he finished lamely.

'Doctor's right, too,' she replied. 'There's no way you're going to be able to play this week. What a time to go and damage yourself!'

'Er, it wasn't exactly self-inflicted,' he said, plucking up the courage to explain how it had happened. 'I did have some help from somebody else . . .'

Elvis cut a miserable figure now, standing near the goal to watch the practice session, hunched deep inside his hooded anorak. He kept trying to give the stand-in keeper the benefit of his advice, but Gary wasn't really listening. He was too busy picking himself up to get ready for the next shot.

The shooters were firing balls at him one after the other to give Gary – and themselves – as much practice as possible. The team hadn't found goals easy to come by since Ravi left and it had cost them dear in the League.

'Watch out,' Elvis warned. 'Look's like Ben's gonna aim for the far post.'

Ben cut in from the left and struck the ball in

his stride. Gary dived the wrong way and the
shot slithered inside the near post instead.

Gary was still lying in the mud, glaring at
Elvis, as Miss Jackson approached. 'You
committed yourself a bit too early there, Gary,'
she said. 'Try and stay on your feet longer – OK?
Up you get.'

The next shot from Henry flew towards the top
left-hand corner and Gary simply watched it go
in. He made no attempt to dive at all.

'Never mind,' the teacher said kindly. 'You
could do nothing about that one. Michael
wouldn't have got near it either.'

She caught Elvis's eye and they exchanged a

grin. 'At least not with my arm in a sling, miss,' he replied.

'It's no use having a one-armed goalie,' she laughed. 'And I'm sure Gary doesn't want one breathing down his neck and putting him off.'

Elvis took the hint and mooched further away from the goal, leaving Gary to concentrate on the continued barrage of shots. He made his fair share of saves, but was badly at fault, too, for some of those that went in.

'Just hope he won't let us down,' Miss Jackson murmured to herself as she watched him in action. 'We'll have to give him as much protection as possible and pray that the Saints have an off day with their shooting.'

'What do you reckon, miss?' asked Ben, cutting across her thoughts.

'Sorry?'

'About Gordon . . . I mean, Gary?'

'Oh, yes, well, I think he'll be all right. He's just lacking a bit of confidence, that's all.'

'Andy Peacock isn't too bad in goal as well, miss, you know.'

She nodded. 'Yes, but we need him more on the pitch. If we take Andy out of central defence to stick him in goal, we've got a double weakness then.'

'Are we going to keep to our usual formation?' asked the captain.

'I don't see why not. Might just have the wing-backs playing a bit more defensively at first until we see how the game goes.'

Ben hesitated before he spoke again. 'Um, can I ask you something personal, miss?' he began tentatively.

'Depends what it is.'

'Well, I mean, despite Elvis and everything, you seem to have been in such a good mood all week.'

'Are you trying to tell me that I'm usually all grumpy?'

'No, no,' he said hastily. 'It's just that some people have said they've even heard you singing to yourself in the gym. We were all just wondering, like, y'know, whether you'd won the Lottery or something?'

She laughed. 'Oh, no, nothing to do with money. I've just won something much more important to me than that – my first cap! I've been picked to play for the England Women's team next month.'

ALL CHANGE

. . . the Saints have no injury worries to disrupt their preparations for the return leg. Everybody is fit and raring to go – well, almost everybody . . .

'Ahhh-chooo!'

Mr Cooper snatched a handkerchief out of his tracksuit top just in time. 'Blasted weather,' he cursed, blowing his nose loudly. 'I shouldn't be out in all this rain, the way I'm feeling.'

The teacher hadn't wanted to cancel the soccer practice. There was so much that the boys needed to work on before the big match. 'You're all going to have to raise your game to beat Lakeview,' he'd told them in the warmth of the changing room. 'A draw's no good, you know that. You're a goal down on aggregate so you've got to go there and win.'

'Are we keeping to 4–3–3, Mr Cooper?' asked the captain.

Simon had to wait for the answer while the teacher wiped his runny nose. 'I think that's the system that most suits us,' he replied at length, snuffling. 'But we've got to put the emphasis on attacking. If we can grab an early goal and put the pressure on them, anything might happen.'

Mr Cooper was hoping that the team might recapture the form and fluency that it was showing before Christmas, but the bad weather was hindering his plans. What began as drizzle had now turned to driving rain.

'Just five more minutes, lads,' he announced. 'See if it eases off a bit.'

His reward for continuing came when a superbly crafted passing move up the left flank ended with Simon and David combining to create a shooting chance for Jagdish Hira. The right-winger only needed two touches. The first killed the ball dead and the second buried it in the net.

'Great way to finish, lads,' cried Mr Cooper. 'That's the kind of football I want to see on Saturday. OK, let's go in.'

The teacher was almost knocked over in the stampede.

Unfortunately, Mr Cooper did not see any kind of football on Saturday. His cold turned to 'flu and he had to spend the next day in bed.

'Take the rest of the week off work as well,' the doctor ordered. 'There's no sense in spreading the germs to your pupils.'

'But we've got an important Cup match on Saturday.'

'You're not playing in it, are you?' the doctor replied caustically, peering at him over his glasses as he wrote out a prescription for medication.

'No, of course not, but . . .'

'Well, then, your young soccer stars will have to prove they can manage without you for once. I am sure there's somebody else on the staff who can take over for a while in your absence.'

Mr Cooper sighed. He knew exactly who that would be.

The following morning in school assembly, the deputy headteacher wished the Year 7 footballers well in their Cup semi-final and then asked the squad to stay behind for a few minutes.

'There's been a bit of a setback, I'm afraid, lads,' Mr Calvert told them. 'We've just heard that Mr Cooper is ill and won't be able to travel to Lakeview – so it looks like I'm your new coach this week.'

As he spoke, Mr Calvert caught David's eye and knew exactly what the boy was thinking. 'Perhaps I'll even be able to undo some of the damage I caused in the first leg, eh?' he grinned. 'Anyway, at least it gives me the chance to try and help St Wystan's keep the cup in the South Quarter.'

'Does that mean there'll be some changes for Saturday, Mr Calvert?' asked Simon, suspecting that the Cup-winning coach might well want to do things his own way.

'That's right, captain. I believe that tactics have to be flexible, depending on circumstances. I usually prefer to play 4–2–4 with wingers, but Lakeview are so strong in midfield that perhaps 4–4–2 might be better.' Mr Calvert paused and let his gaze fall on Eddie Kirk before continuing. 'Whatever happens, you'll be in the team, Eddie. I've seen you perform in Games and can't understand why Mr Cooper hasn't picked you more often.'

The reserve striker beamed. In his eyes, at least, Mr Calvert had suddenly become the greatest coach in the world.

'I'm calling an emergency training session tomorrow lunchtime so that we can start putting a few new ideas into practice,' the teacher finished. 'Be there promptly, all of you, whatever the weather. I think we're going to need every minute we have.'

As the players filed out of the hall, talking excitedly, Mr Calvert reached into his pocket and pulled out a thin piece of paper. It was the teamsheet for the second leg that Mr Cooper had faxed through to the school office the previous evening to be pinned on the sports noticeboard.

Mr Calvert glanced at the names again, printed out in a 4–3–3 formation, then crumpled the paper up and volleyed it straight into the nearest wastepaper bin.

'Goal!' he chuckled to himself. 'I'm in charge now.'

TACTICS

Team tactics may depend upon factors such as type of players available, opponents' style of play, ground conditions and the context of the game. Want to plan your tactics better? Take a few tips from me.

- ✓ Devise tactics to suit the players, not vice versa
- ✓ Adopt a more defensive formation to try and avoid defeat
- ✓ Be more attacking and willing to risk defeat to achieve a victory
- ✓ Plan how to deal with opponents who have special skills
- ✓ Ensure players know positions and roles at set-pieces
- ✓ Ensure defenders know which opponents they are expected to mark
- ✓ Tactics may need to vary for home and away games
- ✓ Plan how to exploit any known weaknesses of your opponents
- ✓ Plan how to make the most of your own players' strengths
- ✓ Plan use of substitutes to cope with injuries or change style of play
- ✓ Be flexible – allow players the freedom to make their own decisions

GET ORGANIZED!

WHO'S PLAYING?

The teams for the second leg of the County Cup semi-final lined up like this:

LAKEVIEW 3–5–2

Bennett

Black   Peacock   Glenn

Vernon   Jarvis   Thorpe (Captain)   Coates   Maynard

Tudor   Singh

James (Captain)   Kirk   Butler   Hira

Melling   O'Leary

Udal   Varley   Bhatia   Rowlands

Brown

ST WYSTAN'S 4–2–4

Substitutes:
Lakeview: Bedi   Freeman   Finch
St   Wystan's: Earl   Witchell   Nixon

SEMI-FINAL: SECOND LEG

(Lakeview lead 1–0 on aggregate)

LAKEVIEW v ST WYSTAN'S

Saturday 28 February
k.o. 10.30 a.m.
Referee: Mr J. Underwood

. . . typical winter football – after the frosts and hard grounds, come the wind, the rain and the mud . . .

'Heads!'
The Saints captain had no doubt in his mind which way to kick. 'We'll have the wind behind us first half,' Simon declared confidently.

'Change round, teams,' shouted the referee, Lakeview's headteacher. 'Blues' kick-off.'

'Best of luck,' said Simon, grinning.

'You don't mean that,' Ben replied, hiding his disappointment at losing the toss.

'Course not. We want any luck that's going today.'

As the goalkeepers passed one another, they touched gloves in acknowledgement and Mark suddenly realized that it wasn't Elvis. He wasted no time in spreading the good news round his teammates.

'That makes our job much easier,' said David gleefully. 'I reckon that Elvis stopped me scoring a hat-trick at home.'

'Perhaps this kid's even better,' replied Jagdish. 'He could be their real number one.'

'Doubt it, but we'll soon see. Let's test him out straight away.'

Lakeview kicked off with squalls of rain blowing in their faces. 'Gotta ride the storm first half somehow,' Ben muttered. 'They're bound to come at us hard to try and make the most of these conditions.'

The two captains met up again very soon. As the Saints launched their first attack, Ben put in a heavy challenge on Simon, knocking the ball out of play and dumping the left-winger into a pool of water.

'Throw-in,' said the referee. 'Clean tackle.'

Simon looked with distaste at the dirty smear all down the side of his kit. 'Huh! Not so sure about that,' he grunted.

The Blues' potential weak link in goal was quickly exposed. As a centre plopped into the Lakeview penalty area, two players went for the ball and it squirted out to the feet of Eddie Kirk. The nervous keeper seemed rooted to his line, as if stuck in the mud, and the Saints' new number ten hooked the ball high into the roof of the net to level the tie on aggregate.

Watching his players' wild celebrations, Mr Calvert contented himself with a little smile of satisfaction. 'Good old Eddie,' he purred. 'Couldn't have started better for us if I'd written the script.'

'One–nil! One–nil!' came the mocking chant from a number of Saints' supporters, but Miss Jackson was irritated to hear another group of lads nearby joining in with it as well.

'Be quiet!' she snapped, making them jump. 'You should be cheering for us, not them from the South.'

'We've come to jeer, not cheer,' answered Ryan cheekily.

'I'm surprised you had the nerve to show up here at all after what you did to our keeper,' she said, staring at Monty.

He responded with a smirk and then suddenly pointed across the pitch. 'It's gonna be two, look,' he cried. 'They must score!'

They didn't. Miss Jackson glanced up just in time to see a shot smack against a post and the ball rebound to safety. Gary was lying in the squelchy goalmouth, helpless, having lost his footing as he tried to take off.

Adam burst out laughing. 'It was worth getting wet this morning just to see this clown they've put in goal. I reckon if the Saints do win the Cup, Monty, they ought to give you a special medal too.'

Fortunately for him, Miss Jackson didn't hear this last comment. She had already jogged away along the touchline to try and reorganize her defence. The Saints were carving them open.

'Tighten up, boys,' she called out. 'Joe, Dan – stay back and mark their wingers closer.'

It was no use. Five minutes later, with Joe snapping at his heels, Simon shielded the ball long enough to lay it off to Eddie who had dropped deeper to support his captain.

Eddie bustled his way past a couple of challenges and tried his luck at goal from outside the penalty area. It was an awkward skidding shot that Gary did quite well to block, but the ball rolled loose and David was on hand to scoop it over the keeper's prone body into the net.

The two strikers had formed a deadly partnership for the Saints, gelling instinctively as if they had played together all season. More goals looked certain. Harry kicked another shot from David off the line and then Gary at last did something right when he spread himself wide and forced Eddie into a rash shot that sailed over the crossbar.

Lakeview had been too busy defending to pose much of an attacking threat, but a lifeline was thrown into their desperate hands shortly before half-time. Ben took a free-kick from near the left touchline, angling the ball towards the far post where centre-back Andy Peacock launched himself forward among raised boots to do a flying header. His bravery was rewarded with a goal as he deflected the ball firmly beyond Mark's reach.

The Blues gathered round Miss Jackson at the interval revitalized with a fresh surge of optimism. 'We'll have the wind and rain in our favour second half,' Ben stressed. 'It's gonna be the Saints' turn to struggle now, you watch.'

Half-time: Lakeview 1–2 St Wystan's (agg: 2–2)

. . . *while the teams are taking a much-needed breather, let's pause the action and turn the Cup floodlights on the two captains* . . .

FLOODLIGHT FOCUS

... on **Ben Thorpe**

school	Lakeview High
other teams	East Quarter Area side
	Medville Majors (Sunday League)
position	centre-midfield and captain
best foot forward	right-footed
age	12 years 3 months
build	pretty average
nickname	only Thorpey
ambition	to lift the County Cup in the air
pets	mongrel dog
family	one older sister
superstitions	always tie my bootlaces twice
hobbies	football
so embarrassing!	missing a penalty in primary school cup final

favourites

school subject	PE
football team	Manchester United
book	The History of Manchester United
TV programme	Match of the Day
music	Match of the Day theme
food	doughnuts
drink	milkshake
word/saying	rubbish!

FLOODLIGHT FOCUS

. . . on **Simon James**

school	St Wystan's
other teams	South Quarter
	Brinkwood Boys (Sunday League)
position	left-winger
best foot forward	left-footed
age	11
build	slim, quite tall
nickname	captain!
ambition	to be a writer
pets	tortoise, hamster, dog
family	no brothers or sisters
superstitions	none, touch wood
hobbies	writing a diary and reading
so embarrassing!	watching video replay of me missing an open goal

favourites

school subject	English
football team	Crewe Alexandra (just like the name)
book	Tolkien's Lord of the Rings
TV programme	any sports programme
music	quite like jazz
food	Indian food
drink	milk
word/saying	Goal!

GAME OF TWO HALVES

. . . with the cup-tie so evenly balanced, the final result is almost too close to call – wonder which team you think will come out on top? . . .

'Pity away goals don't count double, or we'd still have the edge,' said Simon.

As the referee blew his whistle to signal the teams to line up again, the Saints were still huddled around Mr Calvert, sorting out the change of tactics. With the wind now against them, he'd switched the formation to a more defensive 4–4–2, leaving just Eddie and David up front as a twin spearhead. Simon was withdrawn into a deeper role and leading Cup scorer Jagdish Hira had to be sacrificed to make way for midfielder Michael Earl.

'Don't forget to try having a pop at their goalie whenever you can,' the teacher told the players. 'Anything on target has a chance of going in. Good luck!'

Privately, Mr Calvert felt that they were probably going to need it. Although the rain had virtually stopped, the wind had increased in strength and the penalty area the Saints were now defending was badly churned up.

Mudlark Mark Brown was soon in his element. He emerged from a second-minute goalmouth scramble, grinning broadly, with the ball clutched tightly to his chest. His yellow kit looked more like a fancy-dress bee outfit with long black streaks across it where he'd rolled about on the ground.

The Saints put up a tremendous rearguard action in the face of the home side's determined bombardment, often pulling eight or nine men

back behind the ball. Unable to pierce the defensive shield with controlled football, Lakeview began to boot high balls into the box in the hope of capitalizing on some mistake, but such desperate tactics seemed unlikely to bear fruit.

What the tall Saints defenders didn't manage to head clear, Mark leapt high to claim in his safe pair of goalie gloves. But as several players jumped to challenge for yet another cross, a different raised hand appeared to tip the ball away – a gloveless one at the end of a green sleeve.

'Penalty!' screamed the Lakeview players – and so did most of the crowd. To everyone's utter disbelief, the referee dismissed the appeals.

'That was handball!' cried Ben in frustration.

Henry backed his captain up. 'Their guy knocked it away just as I was about to head it.'

'Sorry, lads, I can't give what I didn't see,' panted Mr Underwood, running after the ball. 'Play on.'

Mr Calvert chuckled to himself. 'Who'd be a referee? You do your best to be honest and fair to both sides and you get slaughtered for it!'

Taking advantage of their opponents' temporary distraction, the Saints managed to put together their first dangerous move of the second half. Michael and Simon linked up well in midfield and the captain slid the ball through a gap for David to race on to. The striker carried the ball a few strides and then thumped it goalwards, but keeper Gary threw himself to the left and turned the ball round the post for a corner.

'Great save, Gordon!' cried Elvis from behind the goal. 'I'd have been proud of that one.'

Steve Varley jogged upfield to add his extra height to the set-piece situation and met Simon's in-swinging corner full on the forehead. Gary could do nothing to stop the rocket header, but the crossbar did the job for him. The ball crashed against the Lakeside woodwork for the second time in the game and bounced away.

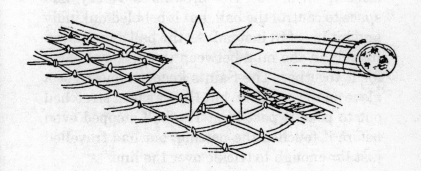

The Saints were caught hopelessly on the break. With Steve way out of position, Ben found the unmarked Jaspal with a long raking pass. Jaspal's loping stride ate up the ground through the mud until tiredness and a covering defender forced him to lay the ball off to someone else, the overlapping left wing-back, Dan Maynard.

Dan was Lakeview's Year 7 cross country champion, and his stamina enabled him to keep going at full steam when others were beginning to flag. He was too wide to fancy his own chances of scoring and he slowed down to check round and consider his other options. There was only one. Henry Tudor was charging up the middle of the pitch, bursting his lungs in an effort to support him.

Mark started to go for the low cross, then hesitated as it veered further away and he found himself stranded. The breathless Henry had space to control the ball, but it bobbled unkindly and hit his shin instead. As the ball spun tantalizingly in the mud between them, they lunged for it together. The Saints keeper almost got a glove on the ball first, but Henry's boot stretched out to poke it past him. The ball stopped even before it touched the netting, but had travelled just far enough to trickle over the line.

'Three–two! Three–two!' went up the chant, only this time it came from the home supporters, enjoying the chance to get their own back on the visitors. The match itself might have been level now at two goals each, but the all-important aggregate score showed Lakeview 3–2 in front.

And that was how it stayed. Despite Mr Calvert changing back again to a more attacking formation in a last-gasp bid for a third goal, the strong wind made it too difficult a task. The damage was already beyond repair.

After the match, the captains shook hands in the centre-circle, ankle deep in mud. 'Best of luck in the Final, Ben,' said Simon grudgingly.

'Do you really mean that this time?'

'Yep, I guess I do. At least we could brag that we lost to the County Champions. That'd be some consolation.'

Ben knew some people who wouldn't see things the same way at all. He grinned as he spotted the little group of Comp players slouching away towards the school gate.

The Saints weren't the only ones to be going home disappointed.

Result:	**Lakeview 2 v 2 St Wystan's**
	h-t: 1 – 2
Lakeview won on aggregate 3-2	
Scorers:	**Peacock, Tudor Kirk, Butler**
Man of the Match:	**Ben Thorpe**

UP THE SAINTS!

Captain's Log – Sunday, 1st March

Bad news! The Log has the sad duty to report that the Saints Year 7 soccer team has been knocked out of the County Cup, losing 3-2 on aggregate to Lakeview in the semi-finals.

In front of a massive crowd in Medville, we put up a great fight to try and recover from our 1-0 home defeat in the first leg. We were actually leading 2-0 at one stage, thanks to goals from the new strike duo of David Butler and Eddie Kirk, but were pegged back to 2-1 by half-time and then conceded the crucial equalizer to draw 2-2.

Sorry, Mr Cooper, this wasn't the 'Get-Well-Soon' message we'd hoped to send you!

In our coach's absence, Cup-winner Mr Calvert took over team affairs. Our bold 4-2-4 formation worked like a dream at first, but letting Lakeview back into the match from a set-piece proved to be a killer blow.

In a wind-affected game, played on a mudheap of a pitch, the second half was a real struggle for us, like trying to battle the wrong way up an escalator when everybody else is coming down!

So that's it, folks. The epic Cup run is over. This is your Captain signing off for the last time – at least until next season!

Simon James, 7C

POSTSCRIPT

. . . scene: Villa Park, a fortnight later. As a treat for reaching the Cup Final, Ben's dad has brought the Lakeview captain and three teammates to watch their first international match – England v Germany . . .

'Penalty!' cried Ben, leaping up from his seat. 'Handball, got to be.'

The referee must have heard him, or at least the thousands of other appeals. He blew his whistle and pointed to the penalty spot.

'Huh! Bet Underwood wouldn't have seen it,' muttered Joe.

'Wonder who's going to take the kick?' said Harry.

'It's Jacko!' whooped Elvis, showing his shoulder had fully recovered by punching the air in excitement.

They were all on their feet now, screaming their support as the England number two walked purposefully forward to settle the ball on the spot.

'C'mon, Jacko, you've got to score.'

'Don't miss, miss!'

'Keep it low.'

A hush of expectation suddenly came over the stadium as everyone waited for the referee's signal. A goal now would put England 2–1 ahead at an important psychological moment, just before the half-time interval.

The boys watched their teacher in total fascination. From a distance, she appeared to be in a little oasis of calm, almost trance-like, staring fixedly at the target and not allowing the goalkeeper's antics to distract her.

'You can do it, Jacko,' murmured Joe.

'I reckon she's gonna blast it,' said Ben.

'No, she won't,' Elvis assured his captain. 'She always tells me not to move till I see where the ball's going. She'll place it, bound to.'

'Right in the bottom corner,' added Harry hopefully.

On the whistle, Ruth Jackson ran in and connected fiercely with her right boot. The keeper dived to the left, anticipating the direction of the kick, but the ball flew dead straight. An ear-piercing shriek of delight went up from the crowd as they saw the netting billow out with the force of the strike.

'Great stuff, Jacko!' yelled Ben as the scorer was engulfed by her teammates. 'What a kick! You wouldn't have smelt that, Elvis.'

'I'd have stayed where I was, not dived out of the way like that.'

'Then you'd have had your head knocked off!' laughed Joe. 'And that would've taken a bit longer to heal than your shoulder!'

'We should've known she wouldn't hit it softly,' said Harry with a chuckle. 'Hard, but fair, that's the way Jacko always wants the game played, remember – straight down the middle!'

. . . *during half-time, the boys' talk turns inevitably to their own big match that's now only two weeks away – the County Cup Final. It's been the main topic of conversation ever since their windswept victory over the Saints. Discover who stands between Lakeview and Cup glory in the next book in the series,* **CUP FEVER** . . .

ABOUT THE AUTHOR

Rob Childs was born and grew up in Derby. His childhood ambition was to become an England cricketer or footballer – preferably both! After university, however, he went into teaching and taught in primary and high schools in Leicestershire, where he now lives. Always interested in school sports, he coached school teams and clubs across a range of sports, and ran area representative teams in football, cricket and athletics.

Recognizing a need for sports fiction for young readers, he decided to have a go at writing such stories himself and now has more than fifty books to his name, including the popular *The Big Match* series, published by Young Corgi Books.

Rob has now left teaching in order to be able to write full-time. Married to Joy, also a writer, Rob has a 'lassie' dog called Laddie and is also a keen photographer.

Have you read the four books leading up to the semi-finals?

COUNTY CUP
Rob Childs

1. CUP FAVOURITES

Quarter-Finals

Four schools are competing for the North Quarter Shield and a place in the semi-finals of the County Cup – the trophy every player wants to win!

Who will be the Champions of the North?

Foxgrove High School
The favourites, known as the 'Foxes', are on the scent of the Shield again . . .

Glendale Community School
An attacking team with a Giant striker – but with a mean streak in midfield . . .

Market Bagley Community School
Playing a sweeper system, the Baggies are in for some Ding-Dong battles . . .

Teffield Community School
Group outsiders perhaps, but playing at full volume . . .

Join the Cup trail and enjoy all the drama – on and off the pitch – in this action-packed series from Rob Childs, author of the bestselling *Soccer Mad* books.

0 440 86383 X

CORGI YEARLING BOOKS

COUNTY CUP
Rob Childs

2. CUP RIVALS

Quarter-Finals

Four schools are competing for the East Quarter Shield, and a place in the semi-finals of the County Cup, the trophy every player wants to win!

Who will be Champions of the East?

Great Danton High School
The God Squad are praying they're good enough to mix it with the big boys . . .

Lakeview High School
Training hard under a star footballer-coach to outdo their Medville rivals . . .

Medville Comprehensive School
Shield-holders, the Comp aim to prove they're still the best team in town . . .

Sir George Needham Community College
Making their debut in the Cup, the College hope to spring a few surprises . . .

Join the Cup trail and enjoy all the drama – on and off the pitch – in this action-packed series from Rob Childs, author of the bestselling *Soccer Mad* books.

0 440 86384 8

CORGI YEARLING BOOKS

COUNTY CUP
Rob Childs

3. CUP SHOCKS

Quarter-Finals

Four schools are competing for the South Quarter Shield, and a place in the semi-finals of the County Cup, the trophy every player wants to win!

Who will be Champions of the South?

Fyleden Community College
Group underdogs on paper, but they hope to bite back on the pitch . . .

Oakfield High School
Red-hot in attack, they're out to set a new Cup goalscoring record . . .

Shelthorpe Comprehensive School
Last season's Cup-winners are desperate to keep it in their trophy cabinet . . .

St Wystan's Comprehensive School
The captain's keen to log some victories to help the Saints go marching on . . .

Join the Cup trail and enjoy all the drama – on and off the pitch – in this action-packed series from Rob Childs, author of the bestselling *Soccer Mad* books.

0 440 86385 6

CORGI YEARLING BOOKS

COUNTY CUP
Rob Childs

4. CUP CLASHES

Quarter-Finals

Four schools are competing for the West
Quarter Shield, and a place in the semi-finals
of the County Cup – the trophy every player
wants to win!

Who will be Champions of the West?

Hillcrest Comprehensive School
Out to show their teacher that the 'good old
days' are back . . .

Kingsway Green High School
Hoping a dash of foreign flair will keep them
on the soccer map . . .

Riverside Comprehensive School
A team of high flyers, wanting to win and feel
over the Moon . . .

Westbridge Community School
It's not only their waterlogged pitches that
tend to cut up rough . . .

Join the Cup trail and enjoy all the drama –
on and off the pitch – in this action-packed
series from Rob Childs, author of the
bestselling *Soccer Mad* books.

0 440 86386 4

CORGI YEARLING BOOKS